Hurray for Barbara Park and the Junie B. Jones® books!

"Park, one of the funniest writers around . . . brings her refreshing humor to the beginning chapter-book set."
                                                —*Booklist*

"Park convinces beginning readers that Junie B.—*and* reading—are lots of fun."
                                    —*Publishers Weekly*

"Park is simply hilarious."
                —America Online's *The Book Report*

"First grade offers a whole year of exciting possibilities for Junie B. . . . As always, Park is in touch with what kids know and how they feel."
                            —*School Library Journal*

"Junie B.'s swarms of young fans will continue to delight in her unique take on the world. . . . A hilarious, first-rate read-aloud for the first-grade classroom."
                                        —*Kirkus Reviews*

"Junie B. Jones is a likable character whose comic mishaps . . . will elicit laughs from young readers."
                            —*The Horn Book Magazine*

"A genuinely funny, easily read story."
                                        —*Kirkus Reviews*

Barbara Park's many middle-grade novels are listed at the end of this book.

Junie B. Jones Is Captain Field Day

by Barbara Park
illustrated by Denise Brunkus

A STEPPING STONE BOOK™

Random House 🏠 New York

With smiles and hugs and happy thoughts,
to a real-life superhero, Andrew Park

Text copyright © 2001 by Barbara Park
Illustrations copyright © 2001 by Denise Brunkus
All rights reserved under International and Pan-American Copyright
Conventions. Published in the United States by Random House, Inc.,
New York, and simultaneously in Canada by Random House of Canada
Limited, Toronto.

www.randomhouse.com/kids/junieb

Library of Congress Cataloging-in-Publication Data

Park, Barbara.
Junie B. Jones is Captain Field Day /
by Barbara Park ; illustrated by Denise Brunkus.
    p.   cm. — (A Stepping Stone book.)
SUMMARY: As captain of Room Nine's field day team, Junie B. Jones tries to
rally her troops after they lose several events.
ISBN 0-375-80291-6 (trade) — ISBN 0-375-90291-0 (lib. bdg)
[1. Winning and losing—Fiction.   2. Kindergarten—Fiction.
3. Schools—Fiction.]   I. Brunkus, Denise, ill.   II. Title.
PZ7.P2197 Jug   2000   [Fic]   00-055305

Printed in the United States of America January 2001

19 2

A STEPPING STONE BOOK and colophon are trademarks of Random House, Inc.

Contents

1/ Chatting

My name is Junie B. Jones. The B stands for Beatrice. Except I don't like Beatrice. I just like B and that's all.

This morning, I woke up very excited! 'Cause today we were having kindergarten Field Day at my school, that's why!

I couldn't stop shouting that happy news!

"Field Day! Today is Field Day!" I shouted to my dog named Tickle.

Then I quick ran to my baby brother's room. He was sleeping in his crib.

"Field Day! Today is Field Day!" I shouted to baby Ollie.

He woke up very fast. Then he started screaming his whole entire head off.

Mother came running right in there.

"Junie B. Jones! For goodness' sake! What has gotten into you this morning?"

I looked at that woman real curious.

"Field Day," I said. "Field Day has gotten into me, Mother. How could you even forget this important occasion? I have been talking about it all week, remember? Field Day is when Room Nine goes against Room Eight. And we have different races and stuff."

Ollie kept on screaming.

"Could you quiet him down, please?" I asked Mother. "He is taking the edge off of my good mood."

She picked him up and patted him.

"Thank goodness Field Day is finally here," she said. "Maybe now we'll be able to talk about something else for a change."

I danced all around that woman.

"We *will*, Mother! We *will* be able to talk about something else! After Field Day is over, we'll be able to talk about how Room Nine creamed Room Eight! Ha!"

I jumped up and down. "You're coming to watch me, right? And Daddy's coming, too! Right? 'Cause Room Nine is going to win all the races, probably. So we will need lots of clapping and cheering."

Mother ruffled my hair. "Don't worry. We'll be there," she said. "I think Grampa and Grandma Miller might come, too."

"Hurray!" I said. "Hurray for the whole darned family!"

After that, I ran out of the room. And I called my bestest friend named Grace on the phone.

And wait till you hear this! I didn't even have to look up her number in the phone book! 'Cause I finally got it memorized right in my head!

Its name is 555-5555. And that was a hard number to remember, I tell you. 'Cause I kept forgetting the five.

I pressed the numbers very careful.

"Hello?" said a voice.

I did a frown.

"Grace? What's wrong with your voice? How come you don't sound like yourself today? Do you have a froggie in your throat?"

All of a sudden, I did a gasp.

"Oh no, Grace! You didn't catch a *cold*,

4

did you? You can't be sick today, Grace! Today is Field Day! And you are the fastest runner in kindergarten! Go tell your daddy that you have to come to school, Grace. Go tell him right now! Go, go, go!"

Just then, the voice talked again.

"This *is* Grace's daddy," it said.

I looked at the phone.

"Oh," I said. "Hello, Mr. Grace. No wonder you don't sound right. 'Cause you are not even Grace, that's why. And so where is she, anyway?"

Pretty soon, that Grace said hello.

"Grace! Grace! It's me. It's Junie B. Jones! I am so glad to hear your voice! You're not sick, are you, Grace? You're still coming to Field Day, right?"

Grace giggled real loud.

"Of course I'm coming to Field Day,

silly," she said. "I *have* to come to Field Day, remember? I am the fastest runner in kindergarten."

I did another frown.

"Okay, here's the thing, Grace. You're not actually supposed to brag about yourself like that. My grampa Miller said that is called 'tooting your own horn.' And it is not even polite."

That Grace did a huffy breath at me.

"I am *not* tooting my horn, Junie B. I'm just saying the truth. We have lots of slow runners in our class, you know. Like Lucille won't run fast because she doesn't like getting sweaty. And you're not exactly *speedy* yourself, Junie B."

I sucked in my cheeks at that girl.

"Yeah? So?" I said.

"So I'm going to have to give us a big

6

lead," she said. "'Cause I'm the only fast one we have."

I made a grouchy face.

"You just tooted again, Grace," I said.

"Did not," she said.

"Did too," I said.

"Did not."

"Did too."

Just then, my mother called me.

"Okey-doke. I've gotta go now, Grace. See ya, friend," I said.

"See ya, friend," she said.

After that, we both hanged up. And I skipped to my breakfast very happy.

'Cause a nice conversation always starts the day off right!

2/ C-A-P-T-A-I-N

That day at school, Room Nine was very excited. We kept laughing and jumping and giggling and shouting.

Me and my bestest friends Grace and Lucille runned and skipped all over the room. 'Cause we had to warm up our muscles for Field Day, that's why!

All of a sudden, my teacher hollered our names.

"Lucille! Junie B.! Grace! Please take your seats right now!"

We stopped real fast.

My teacher's name is Mrs. She has another name, too. But I just like Mrs. and that's all.

"Yes, but we need to keep on skipping,"

I said. "'Cause Grace said we have to warm up our muscles for Field Day. If you don't warm up your muscles, your legs will get clams."

"Clamps," said Lucille.

"*Cramps,*" said Grace.

Mrs. smiled a little bit.

"You girls will have plenty of time to warm up outside," she said. "But right now, we have an important job to do. Right now, we're going to pick a captain for our Field Day team."

Just then, everyone got excited all over again.

A boy named Meanie Jim waved his hand in my teacher's face.

"Me! Me! Pick me!" he hollered. "I will make a great captain!"

"No, pick me, Teacher!" shouted

another boy named Paulie Allen Puffer. "I will be better than him!"

"No! Pick me! I'm the fastest runner in all of kindergarten!" hollered that Grace.

Mrs. sat down in her chair. She crossed her arms and waited for the yelling to stop.

I hurried to her desk speedy quick.

"Mrs.! Mrs.! Guess what? I did not shout just then!" I said. "Did you hear me? Huh? Did you hear me not shouting? I was the only one in the whole room who didn't shout, I believe."

I pulled on her sleeve.

"Maybe you should reward me for that behavior," I said. "Huh, Mrs.? What do you think? Maybe you should make *me* the captain of Field Day. 'Cause that would teach the other children a good lesson, probably."

Mrs. stood up. She walked me back to my table. And she pointed her finger at me.

"Sit," she said.

"Stay," she said.

After that, she went back to her desk. And she held up a little basket.

"Boys and girls, please listen carefully. In this basket, there are eighteen folded slips of paper. Seventeen of the papers are blank. But one of the papers has the word *captain* printed on it. Whoever picks that one will be the captain of our Field Day team."

After that, Mrs. carried the basket around the room.

She stopped at every table. And she let all the children pick a paper.

"Keep your papers folded until everyone has chosen," said Mrs. "We'll all open our papers together."

My stomach felt nervous and jumpy inside. 'Cause I didn't want anyone else to pick the *captain* paper, of course.

When Mrs. got to my table, my heart was pumping very much.

She held up the basket for me to pick.

I reached in real careful. Then I digged and digged all around in there.

Mrs. tapped her foot. "Please, Junie B. Just pick one, okay?" she said.

"Yeah, but I don't think my fingers have touched the right paper yet," I said. "I am waiting to get the right vives."

"*Vibes,*" said Mrs. "It's short for *vibrations.*"

"Whatever," I said. Then I digged and digged some more.

"For the love of Pete!" said Mrs. "Just *pick* one."

After that, I quick picked a teensy paper from the basket. Then I waited at my seat very patient until all the rest of the children picked, too.

Mrs. smiled. "Okay, everyone. When I count to three, you can open your papers.

"One . . . two . . . three!"

I opened mine up.

Then I did a gasp.

'Cause I saw *letters,* that's why!

"MRS., MRS.! LOOK! MY PAPER HAS LETTERS ON IT! IT IS THE WORD *CAPTAIN*, I THINK!"

I zoomed to the front of the room to show her.

And guess what?

She said I was right!

I skipped around in a circle. "HURRAY! HURRAY! I AM IT, PEOPLE! I AM CAPTAIN FIELD DAY!"

After that, I laughed and danced and clapped and clapped.

Only what do you know?

Nobody else clapped with me.

3/ Capes and Lightning

Mrs. hurried over to me. She said to please stop dancing.

"Yeah, only I can't even control my feet that good. 'Cause they are excited about being Captain Field Day!" I said.

I jumped up and down. "I've always wanted to be the boss of these people! And now I am the captain of everybody! *Captain* means the same thing as *boss*! Right, Mrs.? Right?"

Just then, my whole mouth fell open.

'Cause I thought of something very wonderful!

"Mrs.! Hey, Mrs.! Guess what else *captain* can be? It can be the name of a superhero, I think!"

I clapped my hands. "Yes! Yes! I heard of that before! I heard of a superhero named Captain somebody-or-other. And so that makes this job even better!" I said.

I hugged myself real happy. "Maybe I can even wear a whole entire superhero outfit! Like a leotard and tights! And a cape! And a belt with lightning!"

Just then, Mrs. held her hand in the air. "Whoa, whoa, whoa!" she said. Then she quick took me into the hall. And she bent down next to me.

"Junie B., you are very mixed up about being a team captain. Team captains are not superheroes. They're not even close, in fact."

I did a frown at that woman. "Why? Why aren't they?" I asked. "Captains are the bosses, right?"

Mrs. shook her head. "No, Junie B. Not in this case, they aren't. In this case, a team captain *supports* the team. A team captain keeps the team *united*."

She looked at me. "You know what *united* means, don't you? You've heard of that word before, right?"

I thought and thought very hard. But I couldn't actually remember it.

Mrs. explained it to me.

"*Unite* means to join people together, Junie B.," she said. "A team captain keeps her teammates working together in good spirits. Instead of bossing them around, she cheers them on. Do you think you can do that?"

I did a little frown. 'Cause this was not the job I expected, that's why.

Finally, I shrugged my shoulders.

"I guess I can do it," I said kind of quiet. "But I still wish I could have a cape."

I looked at her real serious. "I wish that really, really bad, Mrs.," I said.

Mrs. stood up.

"Well, I suppose if we looked around the room, we could find a towel to pin on your shoulders. How would that be?" she asked.

My eyes got big and wide at her. Then I jumped way high in the air.

"Perfect! A towel will be perfect, Mrs.!" I said. "'Cause then I will look like the real actual Captain Field Day! Plus also,

I can dry my hands occasionally!"

After that, I runned straight to the sink in the back of Room Nine. And guess what? Mrs. found a towel in the cabinet. And it was a red one!

She pinned it on my shoulders.

I zoomed all around the room.

"Look at me, Mrs.! Look at me! I am fast as lightning in this thing!"

Finally, Mrs. grabbed my hand and she walked me over to the door.

"Boys and girls, it's time to get things started," she said. "Let's all form a line behind our team captain."

I spinned around and looked at them. "That's me, people! I am your captain! I am the one with the red cape! The cape will remind you that I am Captain Field Day!"

Just then, Room Nine groaned and

groaned. Only I don't actually know why.

After that, they lined up behind me. And all of us marched outside to the playground.

Then we waited real excited for Room Eight to come out.

'Cause Field Day was ready to begin!

4 / New Thelma

I know two people in Room Eight.

First, I know a boy named Handsome Warren. He was a new kid at school.

I used to love him. Only now I don't even see him, hardly. So he is just Regular Warren, and that's all.

I know another new kid in Room Eight, too. Her name is New Thelma.

The first day she came to our school, my boyfriend named Ricardo chased her all over the playground.

I hollered and hollered for him to stop. But he said chasing New Thelma was fun. And so that is how come he dumped me.

Dumped is the grown-up word for when you have to find a new Ricardo.

Just then, the school door opened. And Room Eight came running out to the playground.

The Room Eight teacher was at the front of their line. She was holding someone's hand.

I did a gasp.

'Cause guess what?

It was New Thelma! New Thelma was the captain of Room Eight, I think!

Mrs. smiled at me.

"Okay, Junie B. Here's what happens next. As soon as they get out here, you and the team captain of Room Eight shake hands. And then Field Day can begin."

I felt kind of sickish inside.

"Yeah, only here's the problem," I said. "I don't actually like that girl. And so I will

just shake hands with the Room Eight teacher instead."

"No, Junie B.," said Mrs. "That's not how it's done. Team captains shake hands with *each other*. It's the way teams show good sportsmanship."

After that, Mrs. marched me right over to New Thelma.

And wait till you hear this!

That pushy girl grabbed my hand without even asking!

"Hey, I know you!" she said real giggly. "I've seen you on the playground before! You're a friend of Ricardo's."

After that, she shaked my hand very hard.

I did not shake back.

Mrs. leaned next to my ear. Her voice did not sound happy.

"Wish her team good luck, Junie B.," she whispered. *"Now."*

I did a huffy breath.

"Okay. Fine. Good luck, Thelma," I grouched.

New Thelma said "Good luck" back to me. Then she tried to shake my hand some more. But I quick pulled it away.

"Don't touch the merchandise," I said.

After that, Mrs. took my arm and we went back to my team.

And guess what?

Just then, I heard my grampa Miller call my name!

I looked up. He and my grandma were coming across the playground with Mother and Daddy!

I runned to them speedy fast.

"Look, people! Look! Look! I am Captain Field Day! See my cape? I am captain of this whole entire production!"

Grampa Miller smiled real proud. Then he picked me up in the air. And he flew me around and around. Just like a real super-hero!

Pretty soon, I heard Mrs. blow her whistle.

Then Grampa Miller put me down. And I hurried back to my team.

'Cause it was Captain Field Day to the rescue!

5/ Event Number One

"CAPTAIN FIELD DAY TO THE RESCUE! CAPTAIN FIELD DAY TO THE RESCUE!" I shouted my loudest.

Then I zoomed and zoomed all over the place. My cape flied in the air behind me.

Those things are marvelous, I tell you!

I ran in and out of all the children.

Then, all of a sudden, Mrs. grabbed the back of my cape. And she held it very tight.

I looked back at that woman.

"Yeah, only here's the problem. I can't

28

fly to the rescue when my cape is crumpled," I said.

"Junie B., *please*," said Mrs. "You need to settle down. No one needs rescuing. I blew the whistle so we can start the first race."

Just then, the Room Eight teacher blew her whistle, too.

"The first event between Room Eight and Room Nine is going to be a team relay race," she said. "Since both of our classes have eighteen children today, everyone will get to run."

After that, Mrs. made a line in the grass where the race would start. Then she told us the rules.

"Each team will line up behind this white line," she said. "The first person in line will run down to the fence, come back, and tag the next runner. The race keeps going on and on like that until everyone in the line has run. Does everybody understand?"

I jumped way high in the air.

"I do!" I shouted. "I understand perfectly perfect! 'Cause I am Captain Field Day, of course!"

After that, I hurried to my bestest friend named Grace.

"You go first, Grace," I said. "You are the fastest runner in kindergarten. And so you have to be at the front of the line."

I grabbed that Grace's hand. And I pulled her to the front.

Only too bad for us. Because Charlotte was already standing there.

"No cuts!" she said. "I was here first!"

I crossed my arms at that girl.

"Yes, I know that, Charlotte," I said. "But I am Captain Field Day. And Captain Field Day says that speedy Grace needs to go first. So move it, missy."

Charlotte stamped her angry foot.

"No! I was here first, I told you!" she said real snappish.

Just then, Grace smiled at Charlotte very nice. And she whispered a secret in her ear.

And then, what do you know? Charlotte backed right up! And she let Grace go first!

"Wowie wow wow! How did you do that, Grace?" I asked. "What did you say?"

That Grace did a shrug. "I just said the word *please*."

I tapped on my chin. "*Please,* huh? I'll have to remember that one," I said.

Pretty soon, Mrs. blew her whistle for us to line up.

"Is everyone ready?" she asked.

"Yes!" we hollered back.

Then Mrs. shouted in her loudest voice. "ON YOUR MARK. . . .

"GET SET. . . .

"GO!"

Then—boom!—fast as a rocket, Grace started to run!

"GO, GRACE! GO! GO! GO!" shouted Room Nine.

Grace zoomed to the fence and back again.

She tagged Charlotte on her hand.

"GO, CHARLOTTE! GO! GO! GO!" shouted Room Nine. "WE'RE WINNING! WE'RE WINNING! WE'RE WINNING!"

After that, Charlotte tagged a girl named Lynnie. And Lynnie tagged Jamal Hall. And Jamal Hall tagged a boy named Ham.

And Ham tagged Paulie Allen Puffer.

Then all of Room Nine kept on tagging each other . . . until finally, there were just three more runners to go!

Their names were Ricardo, and Junie B. Jones, and Crybaby William.

Ricardo made noises like a race car. "Varooooom, varooooom, varooooom," he said.

Then, all of a sudden, he got tagged. And he took off running!

Me and William watched him go.

"Ricardo runs fast for a boy in cowboy boots," I said kind of proud.

Crybaby William pulled on my cape real urgent. He quick whispered a secret in my ear.

"I'm not good at this, Junie B.," he said very nervous. "I'm not a fast runner."

I patted his slowpoke little head.

"Do not worry, little William. I am Captain Field Day, remember? I will save the day," I said. "I will run so fast, you will even be able to walk, probably."

Just then, Ricardo came running back.

"Here I go, William! Here I go saving the day! Watch me!" I shouted.

Ricardo tagged my hand.

I took off as fast as a rabbit!

Then I kept on getting faster and faster and faster!

I turned around at the fence. And I started running back.

Only all of a sudden, a very terrible thing happened!

And it's called OH NO! MY SHOE FLIED RIGHT OFF MY FOOT!

It went way high in the air.

I runned after it speedy quick.

Room Nine shouted and shouted at me to stop.

"YEAH, ONLY YOU DON'T EVEN HAVE TO WORRY, PEOPLE!" I hollered. "IT WON'T TAKE ME VERY LONG TO PUT THIS BACK ON! 'CAUSE GOOD NEWS . . ."

I picked it up and waved it all around.

"VELCRO!"

After that, I put it back on in a jiffy. And I zoomed right back to William.

I tapped him on his hand.

Only that boy just kept on standing there.

"Go, William! Go! Go!" I shouted.

But William shook his head no. And he pointed at Room Eight.

They were jumping up and down and dancing all around.

'Cause guess what?

They already won the race.

6/ Losing

Room Nine was not a good sport to me.

They kept saying it was my fault we lost the race.

I stamped my foot at those people.

"No, it is not my fault!" I said back. "My shoe flied off. And so what am I supposed to do? Run in my sock foot?"

Meanie Jim got close to my face.

"Yes, you looney bird!" he yelled. "That's exactly what you were supposed to do! You were supposed to run in your sock foot!"

I thought very hard about that.

"Well, well. What do you know?" I said kind of quiet. "It looks like Captain Field Day has learned a little something here."

Room Nine did a groan.

I backed away from them real careful. Or else they might tackle me, possibly.

I backed all the way to Mrs.

"They're mad at me," I said. "They're mad because I lost the race."

Mrs. ruffled my hair.

"It's not your fault, Junie B.," she said. "Your shoe came off by accident. And besides, Field Day is not about who wins or loses. Field Day is about having fun."

I hanged down my head.

"Yeah, only what's so fun about losing? That's what I would like to know," I said.

Just then, Mrs. made a 'nouncement.

"Boys and girls, I don't want to hear one more word about winners and losers, okay? Field Day is a day to run around in the fresh air and enjoy the sunshine. We came out here to have fun and get some exercise. And we're not going to care one little bit about who wins or who loses."

As soon as Mrs. walked away, New Thelma skipped up next to me.

"Room Eight is winning," she said real squealy. "Room Eight is beating Room Nine one to nothing."

I made a mad face at her.

"Yeah, only didn't you hear my teacher, Thelma?" I said. "Room Nine doesn't even *care* who wins and loses. Room Nine just came out here to run in the air. So ha ha on you."

"Yeah," said Ricardo.

"Yeah," said Jamal Hall.

"Yeah," said Lynnie.

Then all of those people gave me a high five. 'Cause I made a good point, apparently.

Pretty soon, the Room Eight teacher blew her whistle again.

"The next event will be the softball throw," she said. "Unlike the relay race, this contest is not going to be a team event. The softball throw is for anyone who wants to join in. If you'd like to see how far you can throw the ball, please form a line behind me."

Paulie Allen Puffer was the first one in line.

"I'm a good thrower," he said. "I'm probably the best thrower in Room Nine, in fact."

Lynnie lined up next. "I'm a good thrower, too," she said.

"Me too," said Jamal Hall.

Just then, Crybaby William pulled on my cape. 'Cause he wanted to whisper again, that's why.

"I'm not good at this event, either," he said real quiet. "I don't have to do it, right,

Captain? I don't have to throw the ball."

I put my arm around his shoulder.

"No, you don't," I said. "You don't have to worry about this at all, William. Paulie Allen Puffer is going to win this thing in a breeze for us."

Just then, a boy from Room Eight jumped in line.

New Thelma did a loud squeal.

"Ooooh! It's Strong Frankie! Strong Frankie is the strongest boy in kindergarten!" she said very thrilled.

All of us looked at him.

Strong Frankie made a big arm muscle. It was largish and roundish.

New Thelma cheered and cheered.

"Go, Strong Frankie! Go, Strong Frankie! Go, Strong Frankie!" she hollered.

I tapped on her.

"You are getting on my nerves, madam," I said.

New Thelma giggled in my face.

That girl is a nitwit, I tell you.

Just then, Mrs. clapped her hands together. "Okay, everyone! We're ready to begin! The first person to throw the softball will be Paulie Allen Puffer from Room Nine! We only have time to give everyone one try. So do your best, okay?"

Paulie Allen Puffer did a big grin.

"I only *need* one try," he said. "I have been throwing softballs my whole life."

After that, he picked up the ball from the ground. And he winded up with all his might.

Then—bam!—he threw the ball as hard as he could!

Only too bad for Room Nine. Because

he didn't actually aim that good. And the ball went straight down into the playground.

It made a round hole in the dirt.

Room Nine stared and stared at that thing.

"Bummer," I said.

"Bummer," said Meanie Jim.

"Bummer," said Charlotte.

Paulie Allen Puffer jumped up and down real upset.

"I need another try! I need another try! Please, Teacher! Please! Please!" he said.

But Mrs. gave him a pat on the back. And she moved him out of line.

I walked over to my bestest friend named Grace.

"He blew it," I said very disappointed. "Paulie Allen Puffer blew it for our team."

"Yes," said that Grace. "Just like when you blew the relay race, Junie B."

I made squinty eyes at that girl.

"Thank you, Grace. Thank you for reminding me," I said.

"You're welcome," she said back.

That Grace does not understand sarcastic, apparently.

After that, lots of other boys and girls in our class threw the softball, too.

Roger threw the farthest in Room Nine. The ball went all the way to the fence.

Room Nine shouted his name real thrilled.

"ROGER! ROGER! ROGER!"

The next person to throw was Strong Frankie.

He picked up a softball from the basket. Then he rolled and rolled it all around in his hands. And he threw that thing with all his muscles.

I did a gasp.

'Cause the ball flied all the way over the fence! And we never even saw it again!

Room Eight screamed and shouted and skipped and danced. Also, they hopped and jumped and twirled.

Room Nine slumped our shoulders very depressed.

'Cause guess why?

Losing does not feel joyful.

7/ Skunked

The skipping race came next.

Room Nine chose our fastest skippers.

Their names were Charlotte, Jamal Hall, that Grace, Lynnie, and Meanie Jim.

Those people can skip like lightning, I tell you!

I made up a cheer for them. Its name was GO, SKIPPERS. Here are the words to it:

GO, SKIPPERS! GO, SKIPPERS!
GO, SKIPPERS! GO, SKIPPERS!

I cheered real loud in front of Room Eight. 'Cause I really thought we would win this one.

Only what do you know?

We didn't.

Some of our skippers cried a little bit.

"We got skunked," said Lynnie very sniffling.

"*Skunked* means our score is a goose egg," said Jamal Hall.

"A goose egg is a big, fat zero," said that Grace.

"A big, fat zero is when you're stinking up the place," said Meanie Jim very glum.

Mrs. did not like that kind of talk.

"Hey, hey, hey! That's enough of that," she said. "I'm very proud of all of you. You did your best and that's all anyone can ask. Right, Junie B.?"

"Yes," I said. "Plus also, a win would be nice."

I sat down. Mrs. looked at me a real long time.

"The tug-of-war is the next event," she said finally. "How about another cheer from our team captain to get us charged up?"

"No, thank you," I said. "I already did a cheer for the skipping team. And look where that got us."

Mrs. made squinty eyes at me.

"Try," she said.

I stood up.

"Rah," I said.

"Thank you," said Mrs.

I sat back down.

All of us lined up for the tug-of-war.

Room Eight held on to one side of a rope. And Room Nine held on to the other side.

Mrs. tied a bow right in the middle of it. Then she drew a line on the ground in front of each team.

"Okay, people," she said. "Whichever team pulls the bow over their own line is the winner. Is everyone ready?"

"YES! YES! YES!" shouted Room Eight.

Room Nine just looked at her.

William was behind me.

"I'm not that good at the tug-of-war, Junie B.," he whispered. "I never even did the tug-of-war before."

"Join the club, bud," I grumped.

After that, the Room Eight teacher blew her whistle. And both our teams started to pull.

Room Nine pulled and pulled with all our strength.

"People! People! We're doing it! We're doing it!" I shouted very shocked.

We pulled some more.

Then, all of a sudden, we heard a loud holler.

It was Strong Frankie.

He yanked the rope as hard as he could.

Then Lynnie and Ricardo fell down in

the grass. And the bow went over the line.

Room Eight went crazy and happy. They were loud and laughing.

Room Nine walked to the water fountain very sad.

Then we sat down next to the building.

And we didn't talk for a real long time.

Finally, Mrs. came and got us.

"Come on, boys and girls. There's just

one more event to go," she said.

She took us to the pull-up bar.

The Room Eight teacher smiled real big.

"All right, everybody. It's time for the pull-up contest," she said.

Paulie Allen Puffer stared at her.

"Big whoop," he said.

Then the Room Eight teacher tattled on him. And Paulie Allen Puffer had to sit by himself for a time-out.

Mrs. was not happy with us.

"Okay, children. I understand that you're not in a good mood. But one of the things we learn in Field Day is to never give up. Room Nine is not a bunch of quitters. Are we, Junie B.?"

I looked at Room Nine's faces.

"Pretty much," I said.

Mrs. threw her hands in the air. "Okay,

that's it," she said. "I'm not going to take no for an answer. There must be *someone* in Room Nine who has the spirit to keep trying. Which one of you children has the courage not to give up? Huh? How about you, Jamal? Will you try to do a pull-up for the team?" she asked.

Jamal Hall pulled his shirt up over his face so no one could see him.

"I believe that's a no," I said.

Mrs. looked around some more.

"Grace?" she said. "How about you? Will you try to do a pull-up for us?"

"No, I *can't*," she said. "I really, really can't. I'm only strong in my feet."

"*I'm* not!" yelled a loud voice. "I'm strong all over my whole body!"

Room Nine turned around.

It was Strong Frankie again.

He made another arm muscle at us.

I stamped my foot at that guy.

"Stop doing that, Frankie!" I hollered. "Stop tooting your own horn! 'Cause that is not even polite! And anyway, Room Nine has strong people, too! We have people

who can do a jillion pull-ups, in fact! So there! Ha!"

Strong Frankie crossed his muscle arms.

"Like who?" he asked.

I put my hands on my hips.

"Like *lots* of people, that's who! Like, um, well, like . . . like . . ."

Just then, a boy from Room Nine raised his hand a teeny bit.

"Like me," he said.

Then he walked right up to the pull-up bar. And he stood there all by himself.

I did a gasp.

Then the other children did gasps, too.

'Cause what do you know . . .

It was William.

8/ William

All of Room Nine kept on staring and staring at that boy.

"Look at his little arms," whispered that Grace. "Where are his little muscles, do you think?"

"William doesn't *have* any little muscles," said Paulie Allen Puffer. "I've seen the wind blow him down on the playground."

"Yeah," said Roger. "William doesn't even know what a pull-up *is*, I bet. Our team is going to look worse than ever."

Mrs. snapped her angry fingers at us.

That woman has ears like a hawk.

Strong Frankie went first.

The Room Eight teacher lifted him up to the high bar.

Then, quick as a wink, he did a loud grunt. And he pulled his chin right up to the bar.

"ONE!" hollered Room Eight.

Strong Frankie did another grunt. Then he pulled himself up again.

"TWO!" shouted Room Eight.

After that, he just kept right on going. Strong Frankie kept grunting and pulling. And Room Eight kept on counting.

"THREE!"

"FOUR!"

"FIVE!"

"SIX!"

"SEVEN!"

Finally, Strong Frankie dropped down to the ground.

"SEVEN! SEVEN! STRONG FRANKIE DID SEVEN!" shouted New Thelma.

Room Nine sat down in the grass real gloomy.

'Cause William was next, that's why.

We covered our eyes and peeked through our fingers.

Mrs. lifted him up to the pull-up bar.

It was not fun to watch. 'Cause William just kept dangling and dangling up there. And he didn't even move a muscle.

Pretty soon, Room Eight started to laugh. It was loudish and meanish.

I made a fist at those people.

"Hey! You want a piece of this?" I shouted real mad.

Mrs. snapped her fingers at me again.

Then, all of a sudden, William kicked his legs a little bit.

Then he kicked them again.

And wowie wow wow!

His chin went right up to the bar!

And that is not even the best part! Because as soon as he came down, he went right back up again!

I springed up from the grass.

"TWO, WILLIAM! YOU DID TWO PULL-UPS! AND YOU DIDN'T EVEN GRUNT!" I hollered very thrilled.

William went up again.

My mouth fell all the way open.

"THREE, WILLIAM! YOU DID THREE!"

After that, all of Room Nine springed up from the grass, too.

"FOUR, WILLIAM! FOUR!" we shouted.

"FIVE, WILLIAM!" we shouted.

"SIX!" we shouted.

"SEVEN . . . EIGHT . . . NINE . . . TEN!" we shouted.

William dangled for a little while longer.

Then he kicked his legs one more time.

And what do you know?

"ELEVEN!"

It was the happiest day of our whole entire kindergarten.

When William dropped down, all of Room Nine piled on top of him.

"WILLIAM! WILLIAM! YOU DID IT! YOU DID IT!" we hollered real joyful.

Pretty soon, we heard a muffly voice.

It said, "Get off of me," I think.

Then all of us got up. And we stood William on his feet.

Room Nine danced all around that guy. Also, we tried to lift him on our shoulders. 'Cause he was our hero, that's why! Only our shoulders kept on collapsing. Plus William's shoes kicked us in the face.

Then, all of a sudden, a bright idea popped into my head!

"People! Wait! I've got it! I've got it! I know how to show William he is our hero!" I said.

After that, I whispered my idea to Mrs.

And guess what?

She took the red cape right off my shoulders. And she pinned it onto William's shoulders instead! Just like I told her!

"William saved the day!" I said. "William is our superhero. His name

should be *Super* William, I think!"

William smiled real big. Then he zoomed around on the playground. And the cape flied behind him.

Mrs. smiled.

"See, boys and girls? See what can happen if you don't give up on yourselves?"

Just then, William zoomed back to where we were.

"But I still don't get it, William," I said. "How did you even *do* that? How did you do eleven pull-ups? 'Cause those things are very hard."

William smiled kind of shy. "I practiced, that's how," he said. "I got a pull-up bar for Christmas. And I practiced every day."

Just then, William's daddy came hurrying over. And he put Super William on his shoulders.

Then all of us marched to Room Nine. It was like a happy parade!

And here's another happy thing! Our families came and ate cookies with us. And they were proud of how we did!

My family hugged me very much.

Then my grandma Miller hugged Super William, too. And Grampa Miller flew him all around in the air. 'Cause William loved that cape, I tell you!

And so guess what else?

I didn't even ask for it back. Not for the whole rest of the day!

"This is being nice of me," I said to just myself. "I am being a good team captain."

After that, I laughed right out loud.

'Cause what do you know?

I was tooting my own horn!

"Hurray! Hurray!
Barbara Park
has lots of
funny middle-grade
books, too.
I can't wait
to read them!"

Come visit me
at my
very own Web site!

www.randomhouse.com/kids/junieb

Books are my very FAVORITE things in the whole world!

Read this next book about me. And I mean it!

*Junie B. Jones
Is a Graduation Girl*

by Barbara Park

Holiday Glee with
Junie B.!

It's holiday time, and Room One is doing lots of fun things to celebrate. Like wearing elf costumes and singing joyful songs! Only, how can Junie B. enjoy the festivities when Tattletale May keeps fizzling her holiday spirit? And here is the worst part of all—when everyone picks names for Secret Santa, Junie B. gets stuck with Tattletale you-know-who! Maybe, just maybe, this Secret Santa gift is the perfect opportunity to give May EXACTLY what she deserves.

Celebrate reading at every holiday with Junie B. Jones!

www.randomhouse.com/junieb

RANDOM HOUSE
CHILDREN'S BOOKS

Junie B. has a lot to say
about everything and everybody . . .

young love
Then Ricardo smiled at me. And so he might be my boyfriend, I think. Except for there's a boy in Room Eight who already loves me.
• from *Junie B. Jones and a Little Monkey Business*

girls and boys
Girls can be anything boys can be. 'Cause I saw that on *Sesame Street*. And also on *Oprah*.
• from *Junie B. Jones and Her Big Fat Mouth*

kindergarten
Afternoon kindergarten is better than morning kindergarten. That's because you get to sleep late. And watch cartoons.
• from *Junie B. Jones and the Yucky Blucky Fruitcake*

gargling
I can gargle very perfect. Except I can't keep the water in my actual mouth.
• from *Junie B. Jones Is Not a Crook*

. . . in Barbara Park's other
Junie B. Jones books!

ideas

Just then, I smiled real big. 'Cause a great idea popped
in my head, that's why! It came right out of thin hair!

• from *Junie B. Jones Is a Party Animal*

grown-up words

A *big issue* is the grown-up word for Mother keeps
yelling and yelling and she won't let the matter drop.

• from *Junie B. Jones Is (Almost) a Flower Girl*

arts and crafts

After that, I tried to cut one more heart. But my scis-
sors went very out of control. And my heart turned out
like scribble scraps!

• from *Junie B. Jones and the Mushy Gushy Valentime*

farm words

Pasture is the farm word for big grass and a fence.

• from *Junie B. Jones Has a Peep in Her Pocket*

Barbara Park says:

“I would have loved having Field Day when I was in elementary school.

All that *exercise!*

All that *team spirit!*

And best of all—*NO TESTS!*

Luckily, both of my sons did have school Field Days. Each spring, my husband and I looked forward to going down to the playground and cheering them on. Of course, like most parents, we spent lots of time trying to convince them that it didn't matter who won or lost. 'The fun of sports is in the *competition*,' we insisted.

They didn't buy it.

Neither does Room Nine.

Okay, fine. Maybe losing isn't 'joyful.' But as Junie B. and her class discover, even when things look their gloomiest, life can still deliver some happy little surprises. **”**